MISS SPIDER'S SUNNY PATCH KIDS

For Wisteria

MISS SPIDER'S SUNNY PATCH KIDS

BY

DAVID KIRK

SCHOLASTIC INC.

New York Toronto London Auckland Sydney
Mexico City New Delhi Hong Kong Buenos Aires

"**I**'m not prepared," Miss Spider sighed, and tied a silken string.
"My babies are about to hatch, but I don't know a thing!"
"Relax, my darling," Betty laughed. "It's easy once you start.
The answers will be there for you. They're written in your heart."

"It's time! They're here!" yelled Brother Gus. "They're shaking off the tree!"
"Our Wiggle jiggles," giggled Dad, "and Spinner looks like me."
"Pansy, Snowdrop—tiny twins! They look almost the same.
We'll call you Squirt," Miss Spider smiled. "You have such perfect aim!"

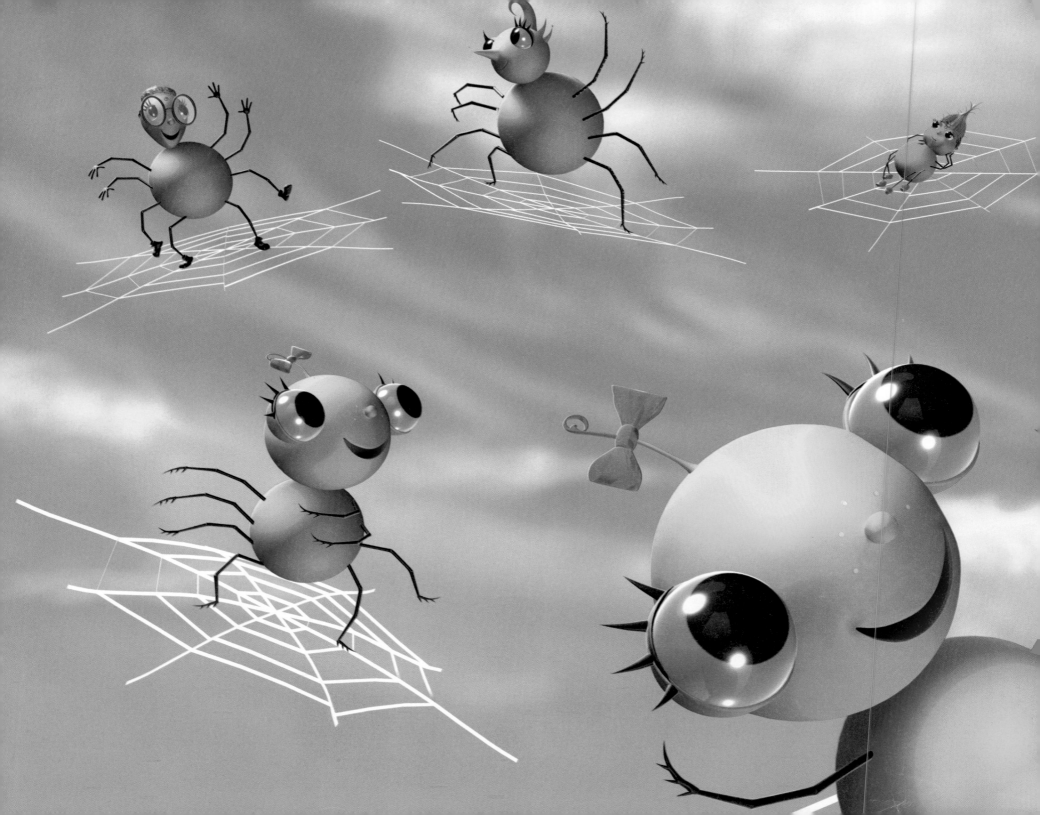

Then out across the treesy breeze, they rode on silken strings.
Swerving, curving, topsy-turving, flying without wings!
Through a pile of crispy leaves, Squirt leapt upon one leg.
Digging down below he crowed, "I found a baby egg!"

"This poor lost egg," Miss Spider said, "belongs to someone, too.
Like all of you belong to me, and I belong to you."
"I understand," Squirt whispered. "It should stay right on this spot,
Unless its mom can't find it here. Or what if she forgot?"

"Don't worry, little egg," Squirt said. "I promise we shall find
A special someone just for you. You won't be left behind!"
With sticks and vines he built a cart to haul an eggy load,
Then rolled his fragile friend on board and wobbled down the road.

"There isn't any doubt," burped Grub, " 'bout where that egg comes from.
Slog down to yonder Snaky Woods! Then, good luck to you, chum!
Of spook-sum places I've been to, that one's the doggone worst.
You'll find the mama there, all right . . . unless she finds you first!"

"Delicious!" hissed a mother snake and grinned a scaly grin.
"It isn't one of mine, but I will gladly take it in."
"You're really very kind," Squirt squeaked. "Perhaps another day!"
And, with his precious egg, he made a bumpy getaway.

"Pansy, Snowdrop, Spinner, Wiggle, children, where's your brother?"
Wiggle hung his head, "He said he'd find his egg a mother."
Miss Spider cried, "My baby! He'll be gobbled by a rat!
Betty! Watch my little ones. Holley, get your hat!"

Lost and lonely, Squirt meandered through the Froggy Bog.
Leaping, creeping shadows twisted in the soggy fog.
All at once, three figures pounced. They dragged him to his knees.
Kicking, squirming, lashing out, he screamed, "Don't eat me, please!"

"We're bandits!" hollered Dragonfly. "Give us your egg, I say!"
"I've got to find its mom," cried Squirt. "Please, bug out of my way!"
"A mother?" Bounce and Shimmer sighed. "We're looking for one, too.
We'll set you free, if you will let us come along with you."

Miss Spider searched beneath each leaf, on every tree and hill. She never stopped to notice how she shivered in the chill. Snowflakes swirled around her head. The wind began to blow. "My baby's not just lost," she sobbed. "He's lost out in the snow."

"What *is* this white stuff," wondered Squirt, "that's falling from the sky?
Like tiny fluffy clouds—oh swat! One poked me in the eye!"
The friends huddled together. Dark clouds eclipsed the moon.
"We must find shelter," Shimmer rasped. "We'll be bugsicles soon."

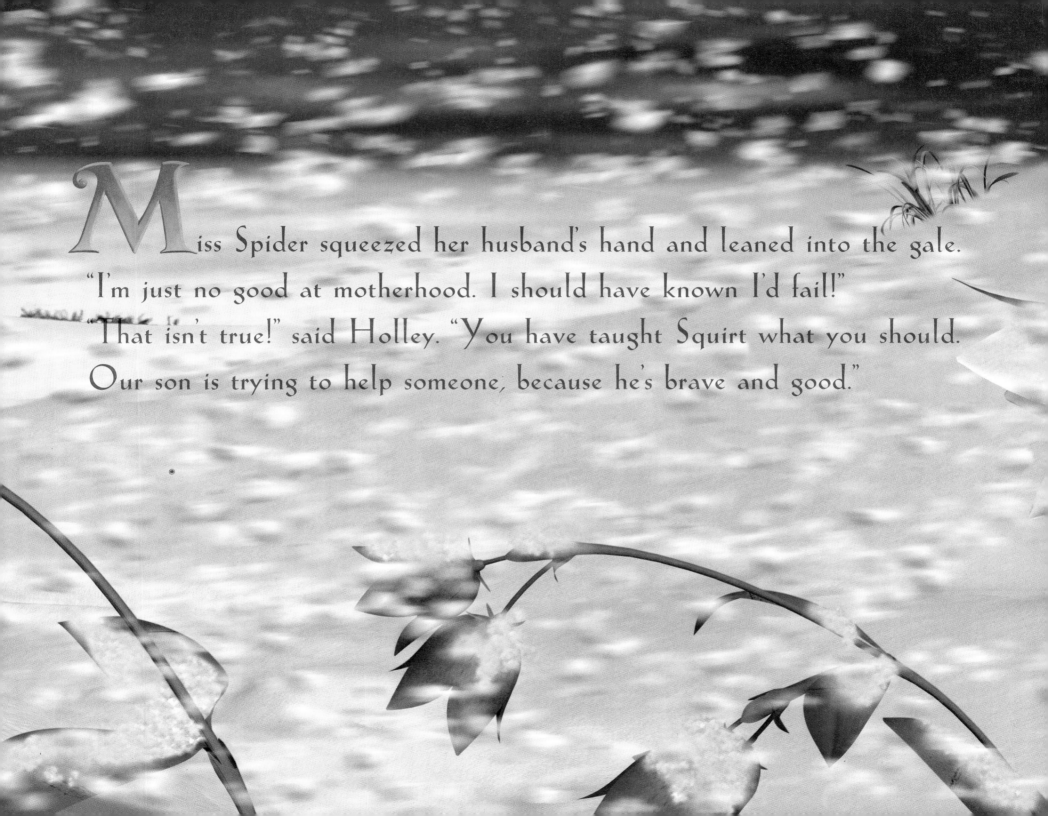

Miss Spider squeezed her husband's hand and leaned into the gale.
"I'm just no good at motherhood. I should have known I'd fail!"
"That isn't true!" said Holley. "You have taught Squirt what you should.
Our son is trying to help someone, because he's brave and good."

"I'm sensing heat," cried Shimmer. "So there must be shelter near!"
Below the snow, up puffed a smell. "Hi, Stinky Stinkbug here!
Please squeeze into my little nook and get out of the storm.
It's dark and dank, but you'll be thankful for a bit of warm."

"I haven't done a thing," moped Squirt, "I should have done today.
I thought that I was being kind, but nothing goes my way.
I make life worse for every creature that I come upon.
I wonder if my mom and dad will notice that I'm gone."

The sun arose on Sunny Patch and smiled away the snow.
Our little friends came up for air, and choked, "It's time to go!"
"It's been a gas!" Stinky exclaimed. "I hope you'll come again!
And good luck with your chicken egg!" Squirt yelped, "It's from a hen?"

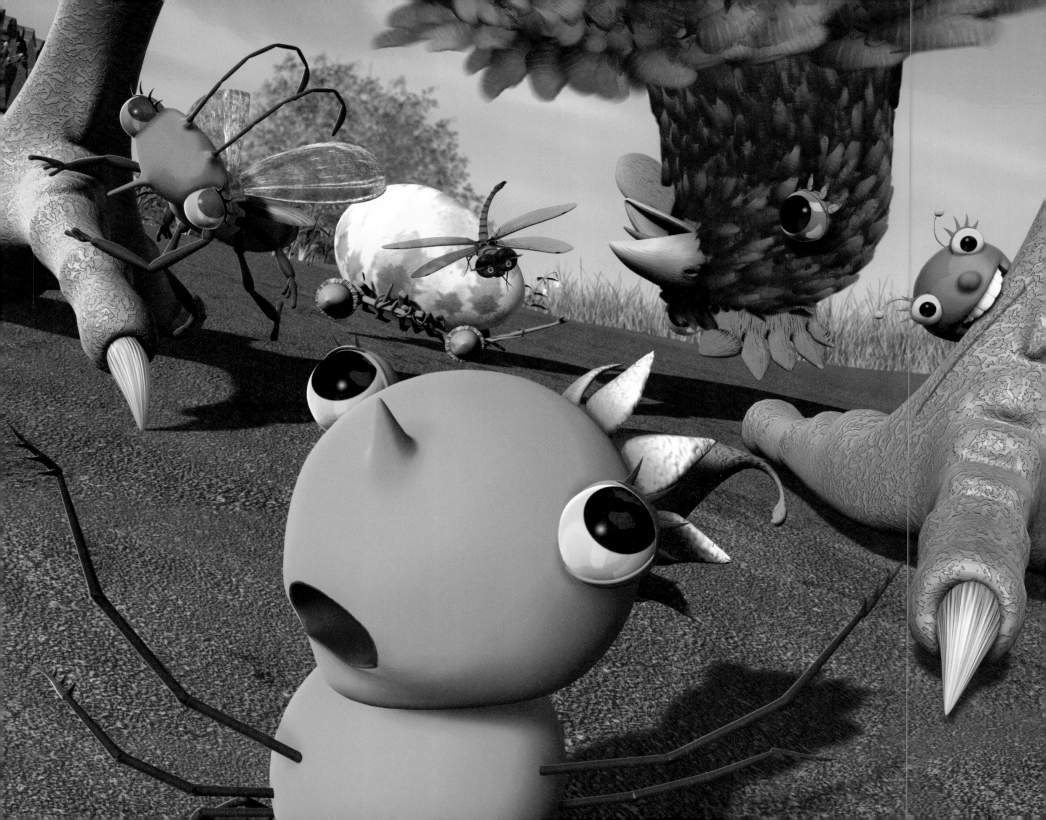

The barnyard spread before them, as they trembled toward the coop.
A hen pecked for a buggy meal. Squirt screamed, "We're in the soup!"
He backed into a corner, no place to hide or run.
Then from the sky Miss Spider swooped and snatched away her son.

"Your mom is sizzlin'!" Dragon whooped. "She's burning up!" squealed Bounce.

"I've never seen a mom with so much wallop to the ounce."

"I'm sorry, Mama," whispered Squirt. "Can you forgive me, please?"

The hen, snuggling her baby chick, clucked, "Thanks!" in Chickenese.

With families back together and a happy end in sight,
Squirt wondered why he sensed inside that something wasn't right.
His mom and dad felt just the same, then suddenly they knew.
"Wait up, you guys!" Squirt shouted. "We've got just the home for you!"

Eight children in the cozy hole—that's how this story ends,
With each of them so different, yet all of them best friends.
Eight children with the sweetest dad—no other dad could match,
And with a mom—the greatest mom—in all of Sunny Patch!

ISBN 0-439-67873-0

12 11 10 9 8 7 6 5 4 3 2   4 5 6 7 8 9/0

Printed in the U.S.A.   08

First Scholastic paperback printing, October 2004

Antoinette White, Senior Editor • Toshiya Masuda, Art Director
Joya Rajadhyaksha, Assistant Editor • Sofia Dumery, Design
Kathryn Bradwell, Publishing Assistant • Raphael Shea, Art Assistant

With many thanks to Jean Feiwel, Barbara Marcus, Jennifer Rees, and Liz Szabla at Scholastic Press

Digital Art by David Kirk and Nelvana Limited

Special thanks to Scott Dyer, Susie Grondin, Paul Teolis, and Gavin Boyle of Nelvana Limited